FRED

Wizard in Trouble!

SIMON PHILIP

Illustrated by SHEENA DEMPSEY

SIMON & SCHUSTER

For Tom, Liv, Sam
and everyone else that knows
Jack Ratt and Big Pete

Chapter One

This is a story about Fred.

Now, Fred looked like any other ordinary boy. He had two eyes, a nose and a mouth on his face, and on each side of his head was a pink, fleshy ear. As you'll know, these features are common. Rarely does a young boy have more or less than two ears, although sometimes you do hear about it. But only if you have ears yourself. If you don't have any, you won't hear a thing.

Like many boys, Fred liked sandwiches. He also liked crisps. And, what he *really* liked were sandwiches made with beautifully soft white bread and crisps that gave a HUGE crunch when he munched them. But what Fred *loved most of all* was a crisp-sandwich crisp sandwich.

If you're wondering how to make a crisp-sandwich crisp sandwich, simply make one crisp sandwich, then another crisp sandwich and then put the first between the second. Or the second between the first. As long as you've made two crisp sandwiches, you can basically do what you like. It should look like this:

Doesn't that look delicious?

Now you know the sandwich Fred liked best, you still think he sounds ordinary, don't you?

Well, he wasn't …

Because Fred was a wizard.

You might be thinking how cool it would be to be a wizard and, in some ways, you're right. Wouldn't it be great to use magic to put all your things neatly away without you lifting a finger? Or for your bed to make itself in the morning because you told it to? For us, yes – but you and I are not wizards, and for wizards completing chores is very basic, boring stuff. It's barely even magic. And, sadly for Fred, his magic was so rubbish that those basic, boring chores were all he could really do.

Well, at least until recently… because just a few months ago, Fred had decided to take his magic into his own hands and entered a competition to defeat a terrifying, fire-breathing lizard and meet Merlin, the greatest wizard *ever*. Which is pretty far from basic stuff. When he'd entered the competition to meet Merlin, Fred had never imagined he'd *actually win*. He'd entered because he was desperate. Desperate to prove to everyone – including himself – that he was worth something.

The months since his triumph at the start of the summer had been the best that Fred could remember. So much had changed that at times Fred felt as if he was living someone else's life. He wasn't used to attention and admiration, but he definitely preferred it to being ignored and overshadowed by his siblings. Before, he'd felt like the odd one out, and a disappointment to his parents. But now he was no longer the family joke. The night after the competition, Fred had crashed into bed exhausted and, with a lesson with Merlin to look forward to, excited by magic for the very first time in his life.

Even so, he'd never expected his magic lesson to take place at Merlin's *house*, or that he would be invited back for tea *every week* throughout the summer holidays. Even more unexpectedly, he found himself becoming Merlin's friend, and finding a friend in Merlin too.

Before his first lesson, Fred's mind had run riot, imagining the things Merlin might teach him. Would he learn to conjure fire? Become invisible? Fly?

Fred had been surprised when Merlin had asked him what he'd like to learn. He'd expected Merlin to just pick a trick and show him. The first thing Fred decided was that he'd like to learn the spells his siblings did to show off. And (after removing several carrots and a surprisingly large biscuit tin)

Fred soon began pulling hats out of the rabbit for fun. Levitating proved to be a bit advanced for their first lesson, but overall Fred was happy with his progress.

Now, though, he could also finally travel between places just by clicking his fingers (the way most other wizards normally travelled), and his improved wandwork made his spells quicker and better too. Fred kept asking to be taught more advanced spells, thinking what fun it would be to disguise himself using magic, change the weather to suit his mood, and convince everyone it was his birthday every day – if such things were possible, of course. Merlin had chuckled sympathetically, and said, slightly cryptically, "All in good time, Fred. There's more to life than magic!" He told Fred that he needed to master the basics first, so Fred practised them over and over – tying his shoelaces, dunking biscuits in tea using only his wand, that sort of thing – until he was more confident than ever before.

For the first time, Fred was enjoying magic! And he didn't have the same feeling of dread that always accompanied the thought of returning to school where all the other students were so much better at magic than him.

In fact, *this* year, he couldn't wait for school to start.

Chapter Two

"Right," Mr Netherboil, Fred's potions teacher announced, "you should by now have a toadstool for your potion."

Fred scanned the room to see if, by some miracle, he wasn't alone in failing …

He was.

Whichever way he whooshed his wand, the toad on the desk in front of him would *not* turn into a toadstool. What was going on? Why wasn't his magic working?

Fred's first day back at school had not gone well. As soon as he'd stepped through the entrance, he realized this day was going to be *interesting* …

The first thing he saw was a sparkly banner that stretched across the entire foyer that read, WELCOME BACK, FANTASTIC FRED! underneath which was a shrine created in his honour (although "honour" was maybe not the right word, as it featured lots of embarrassing photos of Fred, like the one of him on a camping holiday holding a fishing rod, wearing only pants and wellies).

Fred didn't have long to stare at it in horror before awestruck children rushed up to him, demanding autographs. Fred had expected to receive the *odd* comment on his competition win once he returned to school, but he hadn't anticipated *this*. He fought his way through the crowd to find his new form room, trying his best to be friendly and smile while ignoring the uncomfortable tightness in his chest.

As the day went on, Fred couldn't forget that banner. *Fantastic Fred*. He should have been pleased, but he couldn't help finding it scary. Just *how much*, and *what* exactly, was everyone expecting from him? Clearly his teachers were expecting a lot. He'd been moved from his previous class full of toddlers to one of wizards his own age, which was far less humiliating and came as a relief. But it added to the pressure, too.

Worst of all, Fred's magic had been going wrong all day. And now, in his potions class, it had completely deserted him.

"Before we proceed," Mr Netherboil continued, "has anyone *NOT* completed this simple task?"

Fred slowly raised his hand.

"*Really*, Fred?" Mr Netherboil seemed surprised. "What's the problem?"

Fred studied the table in front of him.

"Well, I have a toad … and a stool. But no toadstool."

"You're almost there," his teacher said. "Try flicking your wand, like so …"

Fred copied the movement. The toad did a headstand. Everyone laughed.

He tried again. The toad ended up underneath the stool, which wobbled atop its head.

"Remember," Mr Netherboil said, "it's all in the wrist. Like *this*."

Fred tried again.

"For crying out loud, mate!" the toad cried. The creature looked at its legs, then at those of the stool. They'd swapped places.

"Sorry," Fred muttered.

"You're useless!" the toad said. "I'll do it myself!"

And, with a wet-sounding pop, he did. Where moments before the toad had sat, there now appeared a beautiful, bright red toadstool.

"Excellent," Mr Netherboil concluded. "We're *finally* ready to move on."

Fred sunk lower into his seat. He'd been so looking forward to school. Now, he couldn't wait to get home.

✦ * ✦ * ✦ *

"Here's my hero!" Fred's mother squealed when he stepped through the door.

She drenched her son in kisses. Fred's mind filled with images of toads. He felt guilty for the unkind thought – he loved his mum, and she didn't usually remind him of ugly amphibians. Fred pushed the toads out of his head and his mother gently away in order to catch his breath.

"Come, poppet," she ordered. "My new friends have been waiting to meet you!"

This didn't surprise Fred. His mum had made a remarkable number of 'friends' over the summer, who all seemed to want to meet him. He followed her into the living room, where the gaggle of giddy grown-ups waited. Sandwiched among them were his

younger sisters, Willow and Wilda, who waved cheerfully as he entered.

After Fred had suffered further shrieks and sloppy kisses, he prepared himself to answer questions he'd been asked many times before:

"Was the lizard scary?"

"How did you defeat it?"

"Was the tail slimy?"

"Is Merlin's beard as beautiful in real life as it

looks on TV?"

And some he hadn't:

"Is Merlin single?" one lady asked.

"Is he rich as everyone says?" said another.

"What do you get if you cross a wrinkly orange, a flannel moth caterpillar, a lifetime of lies and an unfortunate political situation?"

"I know!" said Fred. "Donald—"

"What does Merlin's beard smell like?" interjected a fourth.

"Ooh, I bet it's delightful!" one of them said with a sigh and all the ladies giggled, happily entertaining themselves with thoughts of Merlin's beard.

Fred saw an opportunity to be excused.

"Mum, I've got lots to do. Would you mind if I . . . ?" he said.

"Of course not, petal. Silly me – I'd forgotten how busy being a hero must be!"

"Thanks, Mum. But please stop saying I'm a hero. Really, I'm not."

After today, Fred felt anything but heroic. He felt like a fraud. He couldn't do the basic spells he'd managed when he was at Merlin's house – let alone the brilliant magic everyone else now seemed to be expecting of him.

"OK, cupcake," Fred's mum replied.

"Goodbye, Fred!" the ladies chorused together, as he went to leave the room. "Say hello to Merlin for us!"

Fred trudged upstairs to his bedroom. His older brothers were waiting on the landing.

"Watch out, Wolfie – celebrity coming through," Wilbert said sarcastically.

"Been signing autographs again, Fred?" Wolf sneered.

While his sisters and his eldest brother, Wallace, were proud of Fred's new skills, his twin brothers were not. Immediately after his win Fred had briefly gained their respect, but they'd quickly become jealous of the attention he received.

"You'd think Merlin was here, judging by the noise," Wilbert added. "But it can't be. None of us mere mortals get an invitation to meet him, do we? Only *Fantastic Fred*."

His brothers had clearly seen the sign at school and frustration swelled inside Fred. "They're just Mum's friends," he replied. "I'm sure they'd like to meet you too. I can introduce you if you want?"

The twins let out a snort.

"Oh! *Thank you*! So *kind*!" they said. "We'd be honoured to follow in your footsteps."

"All OK here, chaps?" Their father interrupted them, coming up the stairs.

They all nodded.

"Jolly good. Now," he said, handing Fred a stack of old photos, "your mother's asking if you'd sign these for the ladies downstairs."

Wilbert and Wolf burst out laughing. Fred blushed.

"Go on, son. Be a good sport."

It was the last thing Fred felt like doing. He wanted to tackle his homework so he could get on with trying to transform toads again, to reassure himself the day's failure had been merely a blip.

"OK, Dad," Fred sighed. One last batch wouldn't hurt. "But after this pile I'm *not* signing any more."

Fred's dad clicked his fingers and more photos appeared on top of those in Fred's arms. The stack was now higher than his head.

"It's the same pile," Fred's dad said. "And this is the last lot, I promise."

Chapter Three

Fred sank into the battered armchair in the cosiest corner of Merlin's living room, and instantly relaxed. The chair was far comfier than its tatty appearance suggested. Its cushions hugged him in a comforting welcome and the ache in his hand from signing photos the previous evening disappeared, along with the tension from a second frustrating day at school. Fred wasn't sure if the chair was just super comfy or had been enchanted with hospitable magic. Charming chairs to be charming was just the sort of thing the old wizard would do.

Merlin was in the kitchen brewing tea, and Fred took the chance to study the room around him. Merlin's house still fascinated him. It was quirky, but not unsettling or strange, and cosy without being gloomy. Its ancient, uneven walls sloped at surprising angles and were piled high with books, prevented from falling off their shelves only by spellwork. Mantelpieces and windowsills were littered with unusual artefacts and keepsakes. Whenever cold from outside crept through the old walls, the huge open fireplaces suddenly lit themselves, lending a friendly warmth and glow. Bannisters wobbled slightly. Stairs and floorboards creaked. There was a ghost somewhere too. Fred had asked Merlin why he hadn't fixed these imperfections, but the old wizard just said he found perfection boring and the quirks pleasing. Fred agreed that they added to the personality of the house – especially the ghost, who he'd never actually seen but had heard scream "SAUSAGES!" on several occasions.

The kitchen housed a long, solid table, under which Mozz, Merlin's cat, often slept. On a nearby wall was a portrait of Merlin with eyes that seemed to follow Fred as he moved around the room. Tall doors opened out onto a beautiful garden with a beautiful lawn, blanket-soft and wondrously green. On his first visit, Fred had watched with delight as an enchanted lawnmower cut beautiful patterns into the grass and the gnomes who sat in the four corners of the lawn applauded.

"Ta da!" Merlin said, reappearing from the kitchen carrying a tray laden with a variety of colourful teapots. Steam drifted from their spouts and exotic aromas, some more pleasant than others, wafted

towards Fred's nostrils.

"What does sir fancy today?" Merlin said, placing the tray on the table between the chairs. "A nice Darjeeling and Dragonjelly? Snagfoot and Cinnamon? A calming Worplesprout and Wensleydale, perhaps?"

"Erm ... " Fred replied.

"Or might I tempt you with something a little different? Lemon peel and Tigerpuss? One of my favourites, though an acquired taste, I admit!"

Fred pointed at the blandest-looking teapot, hoping the tea inside was equally ordinary.

"What's in this one?"

"Ah, a classic! Builder's Tea. May I?" Merlin offered, pouring Fred a cup.

"Thank you," Fred replied, relieved.

"Sugar?" Merlin asked.

"Please."

"Twenty-nine? I believe that's how it's traditionally taken."

"Just one, thanks," Fred replied.

Once Merlin had settled comfortably into his chair and poured himself a mug of Cherrydust and Ticklewart, he gave Fred a kind but searching look – a look that suggested he already knew what was on

Fred's mind. It gave Fred the courage to ask the question he'd been pondering.

"Merlin, is there a spell to make worries go away?"

The old wizard smiled sympathetically. "Perhaps, but not one that I know how – or would want – to teach, Fred. Magically changing emotions is not only exceptionally difficult, but dangerous too – it's dark magic, difficult to reverse. It's never worth the risk, I assure you."

He saw the disappointment on Fred's face. "You think life would be easier without worries?"

Fred nodded.

"Perhaps you're right." Merlin stroked his beard. "Although, I've always found there are benefits to worrying."

"Benefits?" Fred repeated, confused.

"Indeed. You worry, Fred, but I suspect you think a lot too. Am I right?"

"All the time. Sometimes I can't stop."

"And when you're worried about something, you think carefully about it because you want to avoid a bad situation?"

Fred nodded.

"Does that help you work out what to do?"

"Almost always," said Fred.

"I thought so." Merlin smiled. "Does worrying seem quite so bad, looking at it that way?"

Fred shook his head.

"Good. And I always find the best way to

deal with worries is to share them," Merlin said.

So Fred tried his best to explain all about how his magic wasn't working and how he felt like a fraud who would never live up to everyone's expectations.

Merlin listened patiently and then said, "Well, why don't we practise?" With a simple gesture, he conjured a toad from thin air.

Fred stared at it. It smiled back at him.

"I just couldn't get the action right," he told Merlin, taking his wand from his jacket. "I tried flicking my wrist, but—"

To his astonishment, Fred had transformed the toad into a perfect toadstool. First time. Almost without thinking.

"I don't understand. Why can't I do that at school?"

"You *can*," Merlin smiled. "Magic works best when you're calm and confident. Try not to put pressure on yourself. Magic's tricky and can be easily scared away."

Fred didn't doubt Merlin's words. He just wondered whether magic could be welcomed back as easily as it was scared off.

"Fred," Merlin said firmly, "I have every faith in you. You should too. Remember, there's more to life – to a wizard, to you – than magic. Much more, in your case. Sometimes, even the greatest, wisest wizards forget that magic isn't the answer to everything. Trust yourself. Be kind to yourself— " he clicked his fingers "—and eat some cake."

An assortment of beautiful cakes appeared on the tray next to the tea. Each in turn announced its flavour, as if a tiny person spoke from underneath the icing. As the two of them devoured the lot, the pile refilled, offering them endless scrumptious treats.

“These are magical,” Fred mumbled through a yummy mouthful. “*Literally* magical!”

His worries shared, and with a belly full of cake, Fred went home feeling better. Visiting Merlin was always a good idea.

Chapter Four

"How do you fancy a little adventure?" Marvin asked Fred.

It was Saturday afternoon and the two best friends were sitting in Fred's bedroom. Fred considered Marvin's question. It was because of Marvin that Fred had entered the competition to capture the lizard's tail and *that* adventure hadn't exactly been little...

"What have you got in mind, Marv?" Fred asked.

"Something *very* interesting," Marvin grinned. "I found this in *The Magic Word* yesterday."

Misery at the Museum: Ancient Artefact Mysteriously Missing

The Municipal Museum of Magic is reeling after the mysterious disappearance of a precious exhibit.

Usually displayed in the Ancient Artefacts gallery, *The Trusty Tome of Tremendous Tricks and Splendiferous Spells* appears to have gone missing late yesterday evening. The incident has forced the museum to postpone an event they were preparing in celebration of the magical career and achievements of Merlin, the world's greatest wizard.

The ancient book is believed to be

the only remaining original edition, making it extremely valuable. Intended as a practical guide to magical life, its authorship is unknown.

"The book has disappeared, as if by magic, without a fingerprint or wand-mark in sight," a U.N.I.C.O.R.N. (Universal Network Investigating Crimes of Remarkable Nastiness) official said. "The book was replaced by a different title, presumably in an attempt to hide the robbery. Our examinations of the replacement book revealed nothing magical. We believe it is a red herring, intended to distract from crucial information."

A museum spokesperson offered the

following comment: "Oh dear."

It's not the first time an item has been stolen from the museum, raising questions about security measures. Other items pilfered include a giant's toothbrush dating from the twelfth-century, a gold-rimmed monocle belonging to the Cyclops known as Celia, a centaur's hairbrush and a marble statue of the TV magician Paul Daniels riding a dragon. Several very expensive pencil sharpeners have also disappeared from the museum's gift shop.

The investigation continues.

"So, fancy it?" Marvin asked.

"What exactly?" Fred replied.

"Investigating this mystery, of course! Didn't you read that article? Or were you just thinking about monkeys?"

"I read it," Fred replied, not admitting that monkeys *had* occasionally entered his thoughts. "But isn't it a job for magical-crime experts – like your parents?

"It *is* … in fact I think they're investigating it right now."

"Really?" Fred asked, intrigued. "I didn't think they could tell you about their cases."

"They can't. But I know they work for U.N.I.C.O.R.N. Given what I've overheard and how busy they've been the last couple of days, I think they're in charge."

"Do they have any idea who stole the book?"

"Not yet."

Fred read the report again. *Disappeared as if by magic...*

"Do you really think *we* can help?"

"Who knows?" said Marvin, "but I want to find out. I need a project. I'm *so* bored."

Where Fred struggled at school, Marvin was a brilliant and gifted wizard, who could even teach *their teachers* a trick or two. Fred knew that Marvin sometimes found it as hard being extraordinary as he found it being so very ordinary.

"I *need* to do something useful, Fred," Marvin continued. "Maybe this is *my* chance to show what I can *really* do."

Fred looked at Marvin. His best friend was always there for *him*. He couldn't let Marvin down. And at least it would take his mind off his own magical worries after his difficult week at school. He'd tried to take Merlin's advice and not put pressure on himself, but things hadn't got much better.

"But, Marv, we're just a couple of kids without the resources of U.N.I.C.O.R.N., or their magical knowledge and training. And other than what's mentioned in the article, we know nothing about *The Tome*. Where would we even start?"

"There's the positive attitude!" Marvin joked. "Blimey, Fred – way to put a downer on the whole thing!"

"Sorry," Fred chuckled.

"You're right, though," Marvin said. "We need a strategy. So we'll start by finding out as much as possible about *The Tome*."

"And see where it leads us? All right," said Fred. "I'm in."

"Brilliant!" Marvin grinned. "The first place to start looking is obvious, isn't it?"

Chapter Five

The Municipal Museum of Magic was impossibly grand. Huge pillars rose from marble floors to ornate ceilings. Chandeliers hung in hallways. Visitors stood amazed at the scale of the building and its contents.

Fred, however, noticed all wasn't completely normal. The staff directed groups of excited children enthusiastically enough, but he saw them exchanging anxious looks with one another, as if expecting another disaster at any moment. Stern-looking U.N.I.C.O.R.N. officials patrolled the corridors. The place was clearly still on high-alert. Fred expected to bump into Marvin's parents around every corner. The boys hoped not to, as Marvin was sure if his parents found out what they were up to, they would shut down their investigation before it had even begun. For now, it was best to keep it a secret and if they found anything important, Marvin's parents would be first to know.

The artefacts in the Ancient Artefacts gallery did indeed look ancient. The enormous rooms housed magical treasures from all over the world: weathered wands, glistening goblets and cavernous cauldrons were all displayed in glass cases. In the centre of the room, cordoned off and guarded by a gargantuan man and his gargantuan frown, was a case in which, Fred assumed, the missing book had not long ago been displayed. And this seemed like a good starting point for their investigation. Both Marvin and Fred found it odd that a thief would bother to put another book in its place, rather than simply stealing *The Tome* and leaving. U.N.I.C.O.R.N. seemed to have dismissed the book because it was non-magical, but the boys wanted information on the replacement book too – just in case it proved to be helpful.

"Let's cut to the chase and see what

happens," Marvin suggested. "If you don't ask, you don't get, right?"

Together they approached the case and smiled at the man.

"Hello," Marvin said cheerily. "Can you tell us what's happened to *The Tome*?"

The U.N.I.C.O.R.N. official's gaze

remained fixed on the far wall, his lips sealed.

"Perhaps he's a bit deaf?" Fred suggested. "Speak up a bit."

"COOOO-EEEEEEE! HELL-OOOH!" Marvin shouted, waving his arms. *"OI!"*

Everyone in the room turned to look. The guard raised an eyebrow but still said nothing.

"Marv," Fred hissed quietly. "I said speak up *a bit*, not blow his head off!"

"OK," Marvin mumbled. He turned back to the gigantic man. "So sorry, but we'd really like more information about the theft, and to see what's in the case."

The guard lowered his gaze towards the boys. "I'm not allowed to say anything on the matter. I suggest you go away before I have you removed."

"Now what?" Fred said, as they made their way back through the galleries.

"Let's come back tomorrow and hope there's someone helpful," Marvin suggested.

"Did you get a look at the case?" Fred asked.

"Couldn't see round him. You?"

"Not properly. There was definitely a book in there, though."

As Fred and Marvin headed towards the museum's exit, a group of U.N.I.C.O.R.N. officers filed into a room at the end of a corridor.

The last officer to go inside pulled the door of the room shut behind him, but he was so deep in conversation that he didn't notice the door hadn't quite closed. Quickly, Fred and Marvin positioned themselves as close as they dared, taking care not to be seen.

"It was secured by a very powerful enchantment," they heard an officer say. "But all the staff have solid alibis, so we can rule out an inside job."

"Then we're looking for a very

accomplished wizard or two," a familiar voice said.

The boys hadn't seen Marvin's father enter the room. He must have already been inside.

"What about the book left in its place?"

Fred and Marvin, straining to hear the answer, inched closer to the door.

"*The Amazing Ham Maniac: A Golf Kit* by Evil Ham Erni," a new voice said.

"Ernie with an 'e'?" asked someone else.

"No. Just the 'i'. Why?"

"Just that my cousin's an Ernie – with an 'e'. Rough chap. Thought it might be him."

"Anyway," the first officer said, frustrated by the interruption, "there's nothing magical about it. Total nonsense."

"It appears so," Marvin's father sighed.

Outside the room, the boys smiled at each other. Now they had the information they needed about the replacement book.

"Marvin? Fred?"

Without warning, the meeting had ended and the boys found themselves in front of Marvin's dad as he left the room. Marcus Merry's surprise was matched only by the boys' discomfort at bumping into him.

"Dad! What are you doing here?"

"I was about to ask you the same thing."

"School project," Marvin said quickly. "We're a bit lost, actually."

"If it's the library you're after, it's upstairs," another officer said with a smile as he walked out of the room. "Last time I saw you, Marvin, you were just a wee wizard! I'm

Officer Jack Ratt, but call me Jack. Nice to see you again."

Marvin shook Jack's hand and introduced Fred.

"Ah, of course! Fred! I thought I recognized you. Brilliant job on the lizard!"

Fred mumbled a quiet, "Thanks," as he shook hands.

"Well, boys, we've lots to do," Marvin's father said. "Marv, I'll see you at home. Fred, good to see you."

"Good luck with your project," Jack said as they left.

"Do you think they suspected anything?" Fred asked, once the adults were out of earshot.

"Not sure," Marvin said. "Luckily, it sounds like they've enough to worry about. Now, library?"

"Library," Fred agreed.

Chapter Six

"If you're looking for books on *The Tome*, the last ones just got checked out."

Fred and Marvin turned their attention away from the towering shelves to the gentle voice. They'd been searching for a while. Marvin had tried every sort of book-summoning spell he knew, without success. Then he'd conjured a pair of gloved hands

that began pulling books from shelves at a furious pace. When the hands started throwing copies across the library in frustration, causing several witches to duck for cover, Marvin decided it was best to vanish them back to wherever he'd conjured them from, and the boys quickly returned the books to their shelves.

Now, though, a short, silver-haired witch stood observing them, with a sympathetic smile on her kindly face. Her hunched, slender frame betrayed her elderly years, but the energetic twinkle in her intelligent eyes made her seem far younger and more powerful than her appearance suggested. She peered over the glasses perched on the tip of her nose.

"It appears that everyone's rather keen to find out more about *The Tome* since it was stolen," she said "What *exactly* do you want to know, dears?"

"Everything and anything," Fred replied.

"I see. Well, don't worry about the books. I wrote half of them, so I'm sure I can tell you what you need to know."

"You did?" the boys asked.

"Of course!" The witch laughed. "I may look crooked and old, but I have an incredible memory and I'm considered a bit of an expert on a few things, *The Tome* being one of them – U.N.I.C.O.R.N. are certainly keen for my advice. Though I love being a librarian too. Books are wonderful – to read and to write."

She cleared her throat loudly before

reciting what was obviously a passage from one of her books. The boys listened intently.

"The Trusty Tome *is an ancient work that served for centuries as the chief practical guide to all aspects of magical life. Written to aid the spread of magical knowledge, it contains useful advice in chapters covering a range of subjects: Alchemy and Potions; Broom and Wand Maintenance; Animals and Nature; Hats and Socks; Cooking and Housekeeping; Defensive Magic; and Beard and/or Moustache Grooming Technology, to name a few.*

Supposedly produced by 'The Magicians of Might', a group of elite wizards during the earliest days of magic, its exact authorship is unknown. All but one of the original copies containing every author's name succumbed to the ravages of time.

The one remaining copy went missing for much of the twentieth century, until it was found at the back of a disgraced ex-Prime Minister for Magic's underwear drawer. Fumigated before being sold to a private collector, it remained unseen until recent years, when it was kindly donated to the Municipal Museum of Magic. It remains securely displayed as part of the Ancient Artefacts gallery.

"Or so we thought," she finished.

"Wow, you do have a good memory!" Fred said, before remembering something himself. "Do you know anything about the book that was put in *The Tome's* place?"

"Only that U.N.I.C.O.R.N. found it has no magical properties, so consider it unimportant," she answered, to the boys' disappointment. "Now, dears, is there anything else I can help with?"

"Just one more thing," Marvin replied. "Is there any reason why, other than to sell it, someone would steal *The Tome*?"

She paused, appearing to have an answer on her tongue.

But before she could share it, the old witch was whisked away by a U.N.I.C.O.R.N. official who had appeared from nowhere and needed her urgently.

"Pumpkins," Marvin said. "We didn't even ask her name."

Chapter Seven

The next day, Fred went over to Marvin's house to discuss the case.

Marvin filled his friend in on a conversation he'd heard his parents having the night before. U.N.I.C.O.R.N. were now assuming that the thief was planning to sell *The Tome*, so the agency was focusing its investigation on suspects from previous heists, other criminals who may have heard something, people they knew to be buyers or traders of stolen goods, and private collectors who didn't care if the items they bought were stolen. Apparently, Marvin's father was sure that *The Tome* would prove impossible to sell now that it was all over the news, which meant that as soon as someone tried they'd be able to track them down easily.

But something didn't quite add up for Fred.

"What if U.N.I.C.O.R.N. have got it wrong? What if the thief wants to keep *The Tome* instead of selling it?"

"But why would someone do that?" Marvin asked.

"I'm not sure. But the thief was obviously clever. Other than the replacement book, they left no other clues…"

Marvin raised his eyebrows in a gesture of interest. "Go on…"

"Well, what if they want to embarrass U.N.I.C.O.R.N. or something? Trying to sell it doesn't seem worth the trouble. There must be a different reason."

"Then we'll just have to work out what it is," Marvin said. "Have you heard from Merlin yet?"

Merlin had given Fred an enchanted seashell that he could use to get in contact with the old wizard if Fred needed him. Merlin had an identical one in his house, and to send messages to one another, you simply had to speak into the shell; to listen to them, you held it to your ear when it glowed.

So, as soon as Fred had arrived home from Marvin's on Saturday evening, he had used the seashell and left his message, hoping Merlin would respond quickly.

Fred shook his head. Although he knew it wasn't long since he'd left the message, usually Merlin responded very quickly, so Fred found it strange that he'd not yet heard from him.

"He's an important wizard. He's probably busy," Marvin reassured him,

Marvin was right, Fred thought. There was no need to worry.

Well, probably not, anyway.

Chapter Eight

By Monday morning, Fred still hadn't heard from Merlin. It was playing on his mind, along with the other questions he'd thought about over the weekend. His mind kept wandering off during lessons, which meant he made even more mistakes.

"Fred! Focus!" his culinary magic teacher shouted, while demonstrating the thirteen ways to cook snake eggs perfectly.

Fred tried to look attentive. Unfortunately, his teacher saw he was holding his wand upside down again, and she decided enough was enough.

"If you're not going to be with us in body *and* mind, I'll find another use for you."

She handed Fred an enormous stack of books.

"Take these to the library. Go on."

Fred wobbled his way there, struggling under the weight of the load. When he arrived, he plonked the books on the nearest table and set about returning them to their shelves. As he placed the final book on the correct shelf, the gold-lettered spine of another book caught his eye.

He removed the book from the shelf, brushed a thick layer of dust from its cover and read the title in full: *Mapping Magical History: A Timeline of Publications, Personalities and Principles.* It seemed the sort of thing that might be worth borrowing when conducting an investigation into a missing magical book. Fred wondered whether it was rare too. It was certainly old, and from what he could tell, had never been checked out –

perhaps it was totally unknown. He took it to the library's quietest corner and began to look through it.

Scanning through the pages, Fred found a description of *The Tome*. His stomach flipped as he read about the book containing a controversial chapter on Dark, Dangerous, Deviant Magic. Had the thief stolen it to use this dark magic for evil?

Mind whirring, Fred read on:

The Magicians of Might *were a group of master wizards, who acted as leaders and governors of the magical community during the early days of magic.*

Although the Magicians of Might are thought to be responsible for writing The Trusty Tome, *no official record of the names of the wizards belonging to the group survives. Its exact membership remains shrouded in mystery.*

The only name on the lone surviving copy, though difficult to decipher, is believed to be that of the legendary Merlin, which would help to explain the widely-held belief that he was the most accomplished Magician of Might. Of course, it's entirely possible that 'Merlin' is in fact 'Martin', so the mystery is destined to remain. It is clear that other names once adorned the cover, though it is unknown if these faded over time or were removed for another reason.

Fred read the entry over and over, wishing that he'd asked Merlin more about himself over the summer. He realized now that mostly they had talked about Fred and his magical worries, rather than him learning much about Merlin at all. And why had he still not heard from the old wizard? Had Merlin decided that trying to teach Fred wasn't worth the hassle, after he'd told the wizard about his struggles at school? He hoped not.

Fred flicked through the rest of the book but found nothing else that looked helpful. Still, the Magical Words section was interesting. He hadn't known that 'Alakazam' was named after a wizard called Alan Kazam, for instance, or that a famous witch called Cara Badabra had rearranged the letters in her name to invent the 'Abracadabra' spell. And now he did, which was something.

When the bell rang for lunch, Fred rushed to find Marvin.

Chapter Nine

"*Merlin*?" Marvin said loudly, making the conversation they were having in the quietest corner of the playground a little less private.

Fred shushed his friend and then nodded.

"*THE* Merlin?" Marvin said, more softly this time. "The one you have tea with?

"How many other Merlins do you know?"

"And he's never talked about the Magicians of Might or *The Tome*?"

"Never," Fred replied.

"Do you think the authorities have tried to speak to him? He's the most famous wizard around *and* he's supposed to have written it, so wouldn't he be the first person they'd want to talk to?"

"You'd think so, though it sounds like it's not that well known that he may have written *The Tome*. I'm surprised he hasn't volunteered to help. He must have heard it's missing by now."

They both pondered for a moment. It seemed very strange. Then Fred had a thought that he wished he hadn't.

"Marv, you don't think Merlin could be … a suspect? He hasn't replied to my message yet, and the last time I saw him was

Thursday, when *The Tome* went missing. What if there's a link?"

"No," Marvin said eventually. "It wouldn't make sense. Why would he need to steal *The Tome* if he wrote it? He'd already know everything in it, wouldn't he? And we know he wouldn't practise dark magic – it's Merlin! It must be a coincidence."

"I hope so," Fred replied. "But it's like he's disappeared. I'm a bit worried that something's wrong."

"Fred, it's only been a few days since you saw him. Maybe he's gone away for a bit. I'm sure he'll be back in time for tea with you this week, as usual."

The bell rang for the end of lunch and the boys walked back towards the school buildings.

"What are you thinking?" Marvin said.

"That we need to check in on Merlin. Today, after school."

"Honestly, Fred, you're—"

"I'm going with or without you, Marv. I just can't help but feel something's not right."

The steep path snaking up the hill to Merlin's house seemed never to end. The protective enchantments around Merlin's property meant Fred and Marvin couldn't magic themselves to the front door. The more they walked towards the house, the further the path seemed to extend, until the house felt unreachable, despite remaining in tantalizing

view. It was a confusing, frustrating illusion, designed to make unwanted visitors give up. Had Merlin not explained the enchantment, Fred wouldn't have known to just keep walking. It was the ultimate test of patience and willpower, which the boys – eventually – completed.

Outside Merlin's front door, a jolly-looking gnome dressed as a fisherman sat on top of an upside-down flowerpot. Fred pulled his wand from his jacket pocket and tickled the gnome under the chin. The fish that had hung on the end of his rod suddenly flung itself into the air, landing as a key in the palm of Fred's hand.

"Shouldn't we just knock?" Marvin asked.

"Merlin told me I could let myself in any time I needed," Fred said. "He's a bit deaf so I don't think he'd hear us knock anyway."

As soon as they walked through the door, Fred knew something wasn't right. Everything was out of place: photos hung at strange angles on the walls, furniture was overturned and stacks of paper were strewn across carpets.

He shouted Merlin's name several times. There was no response.

The boys moved into the kitchen. Upturned chairs lay sad and abandoned. A half-eaten meal sat on the kitchen table and shards of broken china covered the floor. It seemed more and more likely that Merlin *was* missing, or worse, had been kidnapped. Why, and by whom, Fred didn't know. Fred's fears began to grow. Anyone able to out-magic and kidnap Merlin was bound to be an extraordinarily powerful wizard.

Mozz emerged slowly from a cupboard. Grateful to see a friend, she circled Fred's feet, brushing his legs.

Fred picked her up. She felt half as big as normal.

"She's hungry. I don't think Merlin's been here for a while."

"This isn't good," Marvin replied.

Fred raided the cupboards for Mozz's food while Marvin searched the house for clues. He returned to the kitchen holding a newspaper.

"This was open, as if half-read. Look at the date."

Fred looked at the small print at the top of the page.

"The evening *The Tome* went missing," he said. "That can't be a coincidence, can it?"

The quiver in Fred's voice betrayed his worries. Where *was* Merlin? And what state would he be in? The possibilities made Fred feel sick.

"I think we need to tell my parents about this," Marvin said.

Chapter Ten

Fred and Marvin tried to read Marvin's parents' expressions as they processed what they'd just been told. The boys didn't know whether to expect a telling off for lying and snooping into business that wasn't theirs, or a pat on the back for what they'd discovered. As it turned out, they got a bit of both.

"You should know better than to sneak around eavesdropping on government officials," Maggie said sternly. "Even if they do happen to be your parents, Marvin."

"I'm sorry, Mrs Merry. We didn't mean to cause trouble," Fred said.

"Fortunately – so far – you haven't. But both of you should be focusing on school, and leave these things to us."

"Mum, you know I'm not learning anything at school—" Marvin began, frustrated.

"THAT being said," Marcus raised his voice above Marvin's protests. "You've done the right thing now by telling us what you've found."

The boys exchanged relieved glances.

"We thought it was strange that Merlin didn't rush to help, too," Maggie explained. "We sent agents to his house. They couldn't get past the enchantments, but from the outside nothing appeared odd. How did you two manage to get inside?"

"You have to keep walking along the path." Fred didn't want to reveal Merlin's security secrets, but he trusted Marvin's parents. "It feels like you'll never reach the door, but you will in the end."

"Right," said Marcus. "And you're absolutely *certain* things were amiss in the house?"

"I've been going there every week all summer. It's always immaculate. And Merlin would never let Mozz go hungry. He loves her too much."

Right on cue, Merlin's cat poked her head out of Fred's jacket. She sniffed at her new surroundings.

"We couldn't leave her behind," Marvin said. "She can stay with us for now, can't she?"

Maggie nodded.

"So, what happens next?" Fred asked.

"We'll send agents to Merlin's first thing tomorrow, now we know how to get in. And we carry on as normal, investigating the leads we were working on."

"And what do *we* do?" Marvin asked.

"You tell us if Fred hears anything from Merlin. In the meantime, you focus on school."

"But, Mum, Dad, we can help! If Merlin disappeared the same evening *The Tome* was stolen, there's got to be a link!"

"Please, Mr and Mrs Merry," Fred continued, "we're sure something bad is going on. I've never been unable to contact Merlin before. We think the thief wants to keep *The Tome*, not sell it. There's a chapter on dark magic, and— "

"Woah, boys – slow down," Marcus interrupted. "We don't know for *sure* that Merlin's been kidnapped – there could be lots of explanations for the strange goings-on. He's a busy, important wizard. Maybe he's gone away, and someone happened to break in. He might be perfectly fine and know nothing about *The Tome*. U.N.I.C.O.R.N. are in the best position to investigate it, so you shouldn't worry. We can take it from here."

"But you've *got* to let us help," Marvin pleaded.

"Marvin," Maggie said. "Investigations aren't easy. There are procedures to follow, ways of doing things. Jumping to conclusions never helps. We know you're bored of school, and we've no doubt you can do this job too someday, but you need to trust us. Everyone at U.N.I.C.O.R.N.

knows what they're doing."

"Honestly, boys," Marcus continued. "We *promise* we're taking your concerns seriously. But try not to worry. It's almost impossible that a wizard as brilliant as Merlin could be taken."

"*Almost*," Marvin said. "But unexpected things happen all the time!"

"And Merlin and I have tea *every* week. He'd have told me if he was going to be away," Fred said. "I *know* something's wrong. *Please* let us help."

Marcus and Maggie looked at each other. They seemed to realize that Marvin and Fred would carry on their investigation, whether they agreed or not.

"OK, we can't officially involve you in

the investigation – but it sounds like you're determined. Exactly *how* do you think you can help?"

Fred knew they needed to consider their answers carefully. This was their chance to persuade Marvin's parents.

"A different perspective might help," Fred said. "We might spot something you wouldn't even look for. I know how to solve problems without relying on magic because I've never been very good at spells."

"And we can do things you don't have time for," Marvin added. "And Fred's closer to Merlin than anyone. If Merlin *is* in trouble, he might leave clues that only Fred would understand."

"It's true," Fred continued. "He *always*

seems to know what I'm thinking. He'd expect me to worry something was wrong if I hadn't heard from him for a few days."

"And Fred does extraordinary things!" Marvin continued. "He beat the lizard, didn't he? And Merlin's taught him loads since then!"

"Er, Marv—" Fred was uncomfortable at Marvin's exaggerations, but he stopped when he realized that Marvin's argument was working.

"OK," Marcus said, after a whispered discussion with Maggie. "But if we say yes, then no more sneaking around. You tell us everything you do. You don't tell anybody else anything. And, Fred, if you hear *anything* from Merlin, you come to us immediately.

Understood?"

The boys nodded.

"Thanks, Dad," Marvin replied, seemingly reassured.

Fred, however, was not. Questions surged through his mind. *Had* Merlin been kidnapped? Was he hurt? What would happen if they couldn't find him? He couldn't help but worry.

After all, worrying was what he did best.

Chapter Eleven

Without Merlin to help him talk through his worries, Fred had decided to write them down. He thought that if he could see them all on paper, they might not swirl and linger in his head. It helped a bit – now he could see just how silly many of his worries were:

- *What if when I click my fingers, I end up floating around in space?*

- What if I get pins and needles and my arms and legs fall off?
- What if I fall fully down a full toilet?
- What if a fully full toilet falls down on me?
- What if the toilet falls down on Merlin and he struggles to teach me properly because he can't get the toilet off him and I stay rubbish at magic for ever?
- What if I misunderstand the spell Merlin's trying to teach me because the toilet makes his voice sound funny and I make all my teeth fall out?
- What if the dentist replaces my teeth with fingers?
- What if the dentist replaces my fingers with teeth?

Unfortunately, it was the rest of the list that bothered Fred:

- Why hasn't Merlin replied to my messages?
- What if Merlin doesn't like me any more?
- What if Merlin's gone missing?
- What if Merlin's been kidnapped?
- What if we never find him?
- What if I'm worrying too much?
- What if I'm not worrying enough?
- What if I'm right to worry, but nobody believes me?

Fred simply couldn't shake the feeling that his worries about Merlin were not as ridiculous as the other ones on his list. And the more he thought about it, the more he was sure Merlin *was* in trouble. Why else would Merlin be impossible to contact? Why would he not answer Fred? Leave his house in a mess, and his cat to starve?

Besides, the only other option was too horrible to think about … what if Merlin hadn't been kidnapped, but he'd stolen *The Tome* after all? Though why would he, if he was one of the authors? And that wouldn't explain the signs of a struggle at his house. Unless he'd set it up, and he was doing it to humiliate U.N.I.C.O.R.N.? But why? What had U.N.I.C.O.R.N. ever done to him? It was all too worrying and confusing for Fred to cope with.

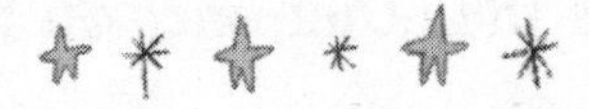

Marvin informed Fred of the latest developments as soon as he saw him during lunchtime at school on Tuesday.

"Every one of U.N.I.C.O.R.N.'s suspects

has a solid alibi. Nobody's heard about *The Tome*'s whereabouts or of anyone trying to sell it. Though I guess that makes our theory that the thief wants to keep *The Tome* more persuasive ..."

"Are they looking into the other book?" Fred asked.

Marvin shook his head. "They don't seem to think that it's important at all."

But Fred was sure there had to be *something* special about *The Amazing Ham Maniac: A Golf Kit*. He hadn't been able to find anything out about it at all, almost as if it had never existed before and had just appeared from nowhere, at the same time as *The Tome* had suddenly disappeared to nowhere. It was too much of a coincidence.

And if it *was* linked to *The Tome*, and *The Tome* to the kidnapper, then figuring out the mystery of the replacement book could be the key to everything – including saving Merlin.

"Marvin, I think we should go back to the museum after school."

"Why?" Marvin's frustration was increasingly clear. "I think U.N.I.C.O.R.N. might be right. The book is not magical, and not important. There's nothing at the library that can help us."

"No, but there's *somebody* there that might," Fred replied. "We've got to keep trying. What have we got to lose?"

Chapter Twelve

The librarian's eyes widened with interest as Fred updated her on the investigation. She pondered her answer carefully.

"I agree, my dears, that it's probably worth looking into that book. Even without being magical, it *could* be a clue. It's all quite puzzling."

Puzzling, thought Fred. *Hmmm …*

"What if it *is* a puzzle?" he said. "I mean,

something that can't be solved with magic. An anagram, or something?"

"An anagram?" Marvin asked.

"You know, rearranging the letters in a word to make a different one."

"But wouldn't U.N.I.C.O.R.N. have tried something that simple?"

"Because there's nothing magical about the book, they've assumed it's not important. Merlin always says there's more to life than magic, but wizards usually assume it's the answer to everything. What do we have to lose by trying?"

Fred looked to the librarian for encouragement. She nodded.

"There must be a spell for solving anagrams," Marvin said hopefully.

"The book has no magical properties so any spell would be useless," she said. "You'll have to do it the hard way, using old-fashioned brain power."

Fred could sense Marvin's disappointment. He'd been hoping to finally put his wand to good use. But Fred was relieved. He didn't think any spell he would manage to cast would be of any help, but he was pretty good at word puzzles.

"Well, good luck, my dears."

"Thank you," Fred said to the librarian, "you've been so helpful. And I'm sorry, we never asked your name. I'm Fred, he's Marvin."

"I'm Miss Badabra," she smiled, "but call me Cara. I'm only too happy to help."

"Arrrggghh," Marvin moaned, "it's useless."

They'd spent what felt like forever staring at the same thirty-eight letters, failing to rearrange them into something that made sense. And time was running out: the library would be closing soon and their parents would be wondering where they were.

"This *can't* be the best way. There *must* be a spell to help," Marvin said and began waving his wand and muttering incantations. Fred ignored him and continued to study the words.

"*REVEAL!*" Marvin said with a leftwards swipe of his wand. "*SHAZAM!*" he shouted, swiping right.

"*SUPERCALIFRAGILISTIC EXPIALIDOCIOUS!*" he shouted with several extravagant whooshes.

Nothing happened.

"*Where's Merlin? Where's Merlin? Where's Merlin?*" Marvin chanted.

And then Fred spotted it. *Merlin!* Using some of the letters, he could spell out the wizard's name!

But there were still five letters left … Fred scribbled down as many words from the remaining letters as he could

Hive

I

Via

Have …

I – have – Merlin.

"I've got something! And someone's got Merlin!" Fred cried.

"What?" Marvin said.

"*Evil Ham Erni is* an anagram. It says: *I have Merlin!*" Fred said.

"That's incredible, Fred! But *who* has Merlin?"

"I don't know. Maybe that's in the other words?"

With renewed enthusiasm they worked on the other words left on the page: *The Amazing Ham Maniac: A Golf Kit*.

"So far I've got *gift*, *flog* and *log*," Marvin said after a while. "You?"

"*Tanzania Magic Ham*. Not it. Keep going."

Twenty minutes passed.

"Anything new?" Marvin asked.

"*Magma, anaemic, might*."

"Hang on," Marvin said, interested. "There's *magician* as well! And *the*. *The – Magician – Might* … we're on to something!"

"And *Of* is in *golf* …" Fred said. "*The Magician of Might*!"

"Fred, you're a genius!"

"We've not solved it yet," Fred said, trying to remain cool, despite jumping up and down inside. "How many letters are left?"

"Nine. Four *'a'*s, *'l'*, *'m'*, *'n'*, *'k'* and *'z'*. What about names?" Marvin suggested. "We're trying to find a person, after all."

"Good thinking," Fred replied and then he remembered the book he'd found in the library at school. He searched the shelves hoping that there might be a copy here too … Fred was in luck. He pulled the book from its shelf, sprinted back to Marvin, and turned to the index of names in *Mapping Magical History.*

"We should look for names with those letters in. Focus on the 'k' and the 'z'. That'll narrow it down."

"*Malcolm Kurtz—*"

"*Alana Mazaki—*"

"There!" Marvin pointed. "*Alan Kazam*. That's got all the letters!"

Fred turned to its entry in the book.

Alan Kazam: Best known as the inventor of the 'Alakazam' spell.

Annoyingly, the book revealed nothing else about him.

Marvin scribbled down the name on the piece of paper, underneath the title of the book.

The Amazing Ham Maniac: A Golf Kit – Evil Ham Erni

The Magician of Might: Alan Kazam – I Have Merlin

"We solved it, Fred!" Marvin clapped. "What a team!"

"We should tell your parents," Fred said,

his excitement fading as he realized that it meant Merlin really was in trouble …

Chapter Thirteen

Everyone sat in silence, trying to comprehend what they'd been told. Marvin's parents exchanged worried glances across their kitchen table, while the rest of the group scratched their heads in confusion. Their own heads, I mean – not Marvin's parents'.

After Fred and Marvin had explained their discovery to Marvin's parents, they had quickly summoned the two other

U.N.I.C.O.R.N. agents working on the case: Jack Ratt, and a man who everyone called Big Pete (big was an understatement: he made the gargantuan man who'd guarded the replacement book at the museum look like a toddler). At Fred and Marvin's request, Cara had also been invited, because they thought her knowledge of *The Tome* would be helpful. Strangely, it seemed that the U.N.I.C.O.R.N. officers already knew the librarian, although Fred and Marvin were too worried about Merlin to ask too many questions.

"It can't be Alan Kazam," Jack said. "That's impossible."

"Why?" Fred asked.

"Because," Big Pete explained, "he's been

dead for almost a decade."

"*Presumed* dead," Marvin's father clarified. He sighed heavily. "U.N.I.C.O.R.N.'s finest agents chased Alan Kazam for years. Most of the time we never got close, then, just as we were finally about to catch him, he died. Supposedly."

"Why were U.N.I.C.O.R.N. trying to capture him?"

"Kazam was one of the cleverest wizards around. He invented spells that other wizards could barely imagine," said Marvin's mother.

"Like in the summer of 1976," Marvin's dad said, "Kazam cast a spell so that all ice cream tasted like sweaty feet."

"*Very* unpleasant," Jack chipped in. "Although he also made sweaty feet taste like ice cream, so it could've been worse. Anyway, there was also The Great Milk Shortage of 1984."

"Lost socks."

"Homework in the summer holidays."

"Homework in the Christmas holidays."

"Homework in any holiday."

"Homework generally."

"Double knots that can't be untied."

"Soggy crisps."

"The handlebar moustache."

"Stale crisps."

"The *pencil* moustache."

"Sticky-back plastic that isn't sticky."

"Tie-dye."

"Itchy underwear."

"Sprouts."

"S.A.T.s tests."

"O.F.S.T.E.D."

"Boris Johnson's hair."

"The accordion."

"Blisters."

"Bunions."

"Boils."

"Onions."

"And," Marcus said solemnly, "the bagpipes. All these evil, unforgivable things, and many others, are magical crimes mercilessly committed by Alan Kazam."

"So why haven't we heard of him?" Fred asked, confused.

"U.N.I.C.O.R.N. have tried to keep his magic a secret. We didn't want anyone getting ideas based on Kazam's spells."

"How did he die?" Marvin asked.

"We actually received reports from all over the world, each giving a different cause of Kazam's death."

"A freak photocopying accident in Fiji, slipping on a banana skin in Sunderland, an ill-fated ironing incident in Iceland, laughing to death in Luxembourg, an out of control pillow fight in Portsmouth and a collision between a cauliflower, kaleidoscope and Alan Kazam in Colombia," Jack listed.

"Any one of the reports could have been true, but it was impossible to prove which of them – if any – was actually Kazam," Marcus said.

"Most of U.N.I.C.O.R.N. were happy to accept that he'd gone, relieved they no longer had to catch him," Jack added. "Others, mainly us, weren't satisfied. We wanted to prove he was gone for good, and searched for the truth. But the fact is, ever since his 'death' there's been no sign of Kazam. Until now ..."

"So Kazam *could* still be alive?" Marvin asked.

"Well, if he *isn't* dead, chances are he's probably alive," Big Pete mused.

"That's how it normally works," Marvin said.

"It is," Pete replied, oblivious to Marvin's tone. "All the people I know who aren't dead are definitely alive, so that's probably true of others."

Marvin said nothing. Fred wondered how Pete had got his job at U.N.I.C.O.R.N.. "Do you think Alan Kazam could have been a Magician of Might?" Fred suggested.

"I think that he very well might have been," said Cara, who had been sitting quietly thinking. "What's more, I think he wrote the chapter on dark magic. In the past, when researching my books, I tried to speak to Merlin about it, but he always politely refused to speak of the matter. That led me to believe the rumour I've long suspected to be true: that Merlin and Kazam were once close friends, before some unknown incident changed everything."

Fred looked at her in surprise. Merlin was so lovely and kind – how could he have been friends with someone as mean as Kazam?

"But why would Kazam steal *The Tome* if he helped to write it? And why would he kidnap Merlin?" Big Pete asked.

"To embarrass U.N.I.C.O.R.N.?" Maggie suggested. "Maybe he's angry that we forced him into hiding. It was that or surrender.

He's got a good enough reason to hate us."

"Whatever the reasons," Jack said, "where do we start looking?"

Chapter Fourteen

The seven wizards frantically searched Merlin's house. It was the next morning and they were determined to find any clues that would help them find Merlin, *The Tome* or Alan Kazam. They left no cupboard unopened and no toilet seat un-lifted. Biscuit tins were raided, photo albums fingered and undercracker drawers ransacked. Socks were sniffed (though nobody was quite sure

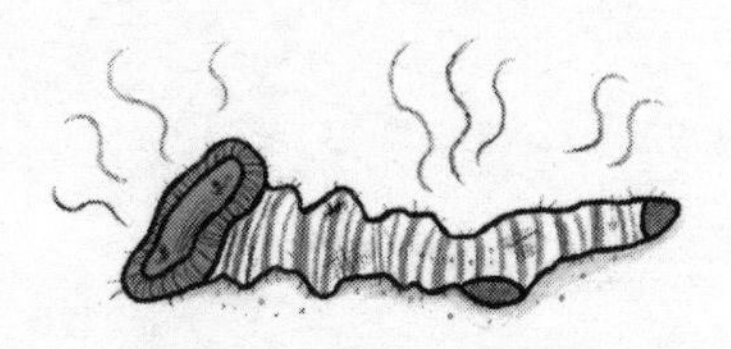

why), bookshelves were scoured, chimneys swept and bins inspected. But other than a preposterous pair of pink polka-dot bloomers and a curious collection of rubber ducks, nothing of interest was found.

As the others took a moment's rest around the kitchen table, Fred inspected the portrait of Merlin. Something about it was different. Today, the eyes weren't just following him; they seemed to be speaking to Fred, encouraging him to look closer.

Fred ran his fingers around the frame of the painting. Was he imagining things? *Surely* Merlin's portrait hadn't just winked at him? He started to prise it from the wall…

"Look!" Fred cried, nodding at where the picture had been. Set deep into the wall was what looked like a safe, now exposed for everyone to see.

Marvin's father studied it, then ordered everyone to stand back. With a single tap of his wand the safe door flung open.

He laid its contents on the kitchen table. Everyone craned their necks to have a closer look at the objects in front of them.

"Merlin really does love rubber ducks, doesn't he?" Jack said, bewildered. "Why would he keep them in a safe?"

"Never mind that. Look …" Marcus said as he pulled a map from an envelope. It was weathered with age and curling at the edges and what little was marked on it was faded and almost invisible. Yet there remained faint traces of some sort of settlement, and lines showing a barren, mountainous landscape, littered with caves and boulder-strewn valleys. Among them, a miniscule 'X' drawn in pale red ink marked the spot of something, though exactly what or where wasn't obvious.

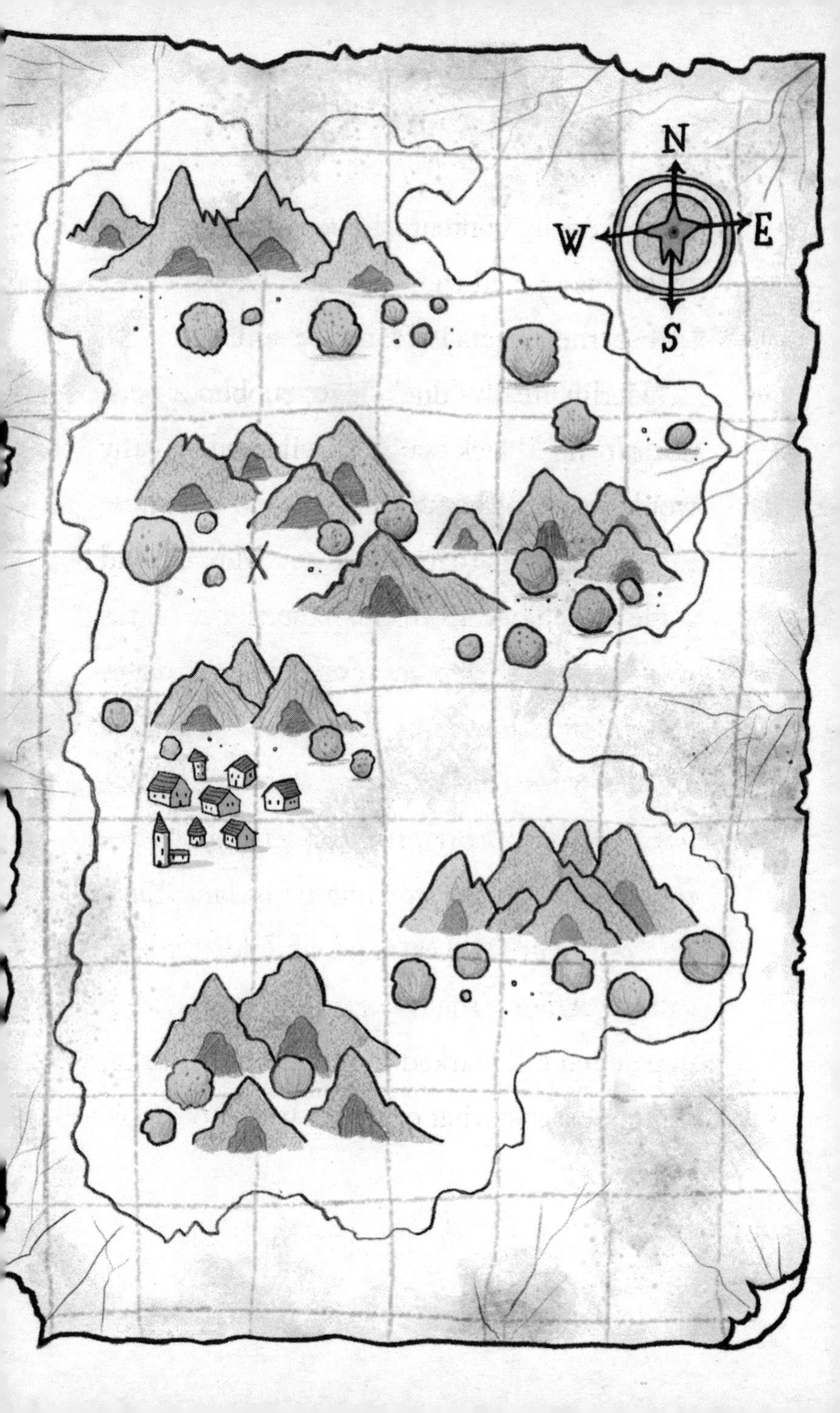
N
W
E
S
X

The group passed the map around the table.

It seemed strangely familiar to Fred…

"This is interesting," Marcus, who'd been examining the other items from the safe, suddenly said. "It's part of a letter. From the same envelope as the map."

He read aloud from the paper:

"I leave you a reminder of where we once were, but our paths must now diverge. It didn't have to end like this, but you've made your decision – one that I'll make you regret. I've forgiven you many things in the past. This I cannot. You'll find this is my final letter to you. Until we meet again, goodbye.

A.K."

"A.K. – that's got to be Kazam!" Marvin said.

"So they *were* friends. I wonder what Merlin did," Jack said. "Maybe he isn't as squeaky-clean as we've always thought. You know him best, Fred – any ideas?"

Fred was watching Cara, who had turned over the map.

"*M.o.M.– D.D.* – what does that mean?" she said, pointing to the initials scribbled on the otherwise blank side of the map.

"Magicians of Might?" Maggie said. "But *D.D.*?

"Donald Duck?" Jack suggested.

"David Dickinson, the antiques expert – the map might be his?" Big Pete offered.

"Both unlikely. What about places?"

"Dawlish in Devon?"

"Dorchester, Dorset?"

"Durdle Door?"

And then Fred realized why the map was familiar. He *had* been to the dramatic place where jagged mountains rose from valleys scattered with rocks, and where dark, cavernous caves housed terrifying monsters with magic in their fiery breath.

"Death's Door!" he said. "It's a map of Death's Door!"

Chapter Fifteen

The group scrambled towards the base of the monstrous mountains that marked out Death's Door as a place like no other. On Fred's advice (based on experience of his previous trip to Death's Door), the group hastily packed their bags with any item – no matter how odd – they thought they might need. Then, one by one they'd clicked themselves there. Even Fred managed to control his nerves and make the simple spell work.

Fred and Marvin had expected to have to fight to accompany the group (not least because they'd be missing school) but it turned out that the U.N.I.C.O.R.N. team *wanted* them to come. Not only because it was Fred and Marvin's investigation that had got them this far, but also because Fred's friendship with Merlin and knowledge of Death's Door were bound to be helpful, and Marvin's advanced magic would definitely be needed. Besides, Fred and Marvin came as a team. They needed each other, and the others needed them.

They'd decided to head for the spot marked 'X' on the map, assuming that it held some importance to the Magicians of Might, and therefore Merlin and Kazam. They guessed 'X' would be some kind of cave where Kazam could hide, but the map was so faded that it wasn't obvious exactly where 'X' was so they were forced to search for it on foot rather than being able to 'click' themselves there.

At the front of the group Big Pete's colossal figure shielded Fred as Fred tried to guide them towards the caves. It was only a month or so since Fred had faced the lizard here, but his memory of the place was hazy, though the familiar feeling of fear and hopelessness that flooded over him now was pin-sharp.

To Fred's right was Marvin; to his left, Jack. Cara, despite her age, moved nimbly behind, as if gliding across the ground. Next to her was Marvin's mother, wand raised high above her head, concentrating with fierce determination. Her husband brought up the rear, scanning the surroundings.

Fred glanced at the ancient map, then tapped Big Pete on the shoulder. They changed direction.

Suddenly the afternoon sun disappeared from the sky. The group huddled together as, suddenly, enormous, icy raindrops lashed

down, thudding against the granite boulders that lay on the ground. Lightning flashed across the dark, malicious sky.

"What is going on with the weather?" Marvin shouted against the thunder.

"It feels like a protective enchantment," Cara said sombrely. "To deter us."

"Does that mean we're close?" Fred asked.

"Kazam probably expected visitors eventually, and wants to make things difficult. This might help." Cara moved her wand in an elegant circle around her head. The raindrops now stopped a few metres in front of them and fell with a calming pitter-patter, rather than the thump of before. Fred felt warmth slowly return to his bones as he marvelled at the invisible bubble that Cara had cast around them.

"It won't hold for ever," she said, "but for now it'll do."

They walked on. Eventually, the thunder and lightning stopped, but the gale and deluge surged on, until it was raining cats and dogs – *literally*. Startled tabbies fell from the sky, bouncing off the protective shield. Great Danes tumbled down and bumped off the bubble, which sagged more with each impact. Basset Hounds' ears flapped as they fell, while drool from the Boxers' jowls caused a downpour of its own as the dogs sped through the air.

"The bubble won't hold much longer," Cara explained. "We need to shelter somewhere else."

"Quick – in here!" Maggie gestured,

ducking into a cave as the bubble burst. The others followed, narrowly avoiding a falling Jack Russell.

Fred watched as the torrent of tabbies and deluge of dogs slowed, wondering what else lay in wait for them. His fear grew as he realized what they were up against; a deranged, unpredictable wizard with a weird sense of humour. He fought the urge to write 'deranged wizard' on his worry list. Writing a list *now* would look ridiculous. Fred could feel himself worrying about worrying, then worrying about worrying about worrying.

From the dark depths of the cave suddenly came a slow, rhythmical *THOMP – THOMP – THOMP – THOMP* followed by a sliding, rustling noise. Something enormous was plodding, then slithering towards them.

"What was *THAT*?" Jack asked.

"I don't like this," Big Pete said shakily.

“Let’s move,” Marcus ordered, dragging everyone towards the mouth of the cave. “Quickly!”

The sound grew louder. Closer.

“Marvin, hurry up!” Marcus shouted.

THOMP – THOMP –

“Pete, run!”

THOMP – THOMP –

“Fred – dive!”

A scorching jet of golden fire narrowly missed Fred’s bottom. He picked himself off

the rocky ground and sprinted from the cave. He didn't stop to look back at the marbled, lava-like eyes that were shining from within it, or the creature they belonged to.

After all, they were already seared into his memory. Now wasn't the time for a chat.

Chapter Sixteen

Exhausted, the group staggered on. They consulted the map at each cave they came to, hoping to find the place marked by the tiny red 'X', but the terrain was so similar they were never quite sure where they were. With each step they felt further away from success.

"We're going in circles," Big Pete said.

"Or we're in the wrong place altogether."

Jack yanked the map from Pete's hands. "Maybe D.D. stands for something else."

But Fred wasn't listening. He carried on walking towards an odd-looking patch of mountainside ahead. As he got closer, he realized the rock had been shifted somehow and there was a tiny hole that went deep into the rock face. He was sure he could hear a muffled sound coming from within.

He called the others over to listen too, but no one could make it out clearly.

"I've got an idea," Marvin said. He flicked his wand at each of them in turn, then stood back to admire his work. "That should help."

"What have you done?" Big Pete grimaced. His ears were more enormous than ever. They'd quadrupled in size, as had everyone's.

"I've always wanted to try that spell," Marvin grinned. "Try listening again."

They pressed their ridiculous ears against the mountainside. The sound was clear, magnified by Marvin's enchantment.

Maggie seemed shocked. "That sounds like…"

"*Alan Kazam*," Marcus said. "It's his voice. I know it."

"How do we get to him?" Pete said.

"Through there." Cara gestured in the direction of the tiny hole in the rock face.

"We can't fit through there!" Pete said disbelievingly.

The old witch pointed her wand at the miniscule gap in the mountain and rotated it slowly. As she did so, the hole spiralled outwards until a tunnel gradually appeared, wide enough for them all.

"Better?" She raised her eyebrows at Pete, who obediently resumed his place at the front of the group.

"Stay in formation," Marcus ordered. "Be ready. He might have realized we're here, and be waiting."

Together, they stepped inside.

When the dank, shadowy tunnel eventually reached a bend, Pete came to a halt and held up his hand. Everyone stopped and peered round the corner.

The tunnel opened into a vast chamber. Sharp stalactites hung from the ceiling, looming like daggers waiting to be dropped. Fires mounted high on the walls cast a mesmerising light that flickered across the cave. Fred's eyes followed the light to a figure in the middle of the room.

At first glance, it looked like Merlin; dazzling white hair, slender frame, an elegance that hinted at a fabulous style of magic. But as the light fell upon the wizard's face, Fred saw that behind his eyes was not kindness but menace. It had to be Kazam!

In front of the wizard, a hefty book stood on a plinth. Kazam muttered as he traced his wand along its spine, gold letters shimmering in the dancing firelight.

"That's it," Cara whispered. "*The Trusty Tome.*"

And then Fred saw something terrible. Across the chamber, just beyond Kazam, was a tremendous slab of glistening ice. Staring out from inside it, unmoving – his brilliant turquoise eyes wide open – was Merlin.

Chapter Seventeen

Marcus turned to Cara.

"Can you stop Kazam getting out?"

"Yes, but it will stop us leaving that way too."

"Do it," Marcus said. Cara set about enchanting the chamber to prevent anyone disappearing by 'click', while Marcus addressed the others.

"Here's the plan. Mags, you're with me.

Jack, Pete – see that ridge that runs in front of the wall? Keep low and use it to get to Merlin while we distract Kazam. Do whatever you must to free Merlin. We'll buy you as much time as we can."

Marcus turned to Marvin and Fred.

"Boys, this is dangerous, so we've got to be clever. You should stay here with Cara. None of you officially work for U.N.I.C.O.R.N. so it's better that way. If we need help, you can be our back-up, but don't move unless I say so. You're our secret weapon, okay? He won't be expecting reinforcements. If we get into trouble, do what you must. Understood?"

The boys nodded. Fred could tell Marvin desperately wanted to be in the action but knew this wasn't the time to argue with his dad. Now that they'd seen what Kazam had done to Merlin, they were *truly* frightened. How could a wizard this powerful possibly be defeated? They had to hope that Merlin's downfall had been because he'd been alone, that together, as a team, they'd stand a better chance. But all the boys could do now was watch nervously alongside Cara as the other four tiptoed around the cave. Miraculously, Jack and Big Pete stayed out of Kazam's sight and took cover close to Merlin's icy prison.

As Marvin's parents crept in the opposite direction towards him, unnoticed, Kazam directed more spells at *The Tome*.

"What ghastly magic *is* this?!" he yelled as scarlet sparks shot angrily from his wand. "Days of trying, yet it still resists my magic!"

As he grew ever angrier, Marvin's parents tiptoed ever closer towards him …

"How can a book not recognize its *true* maker, even in the place where it was made?" Kazam paused, composing himself. "*Unless* …"

That must be why the cave is important, Fred thought. The Tome *was written here!*

Then, after dragging his wand across his open palm, Kazam stepped forward and placed his now wounded hand on *The Tome*. To Fred's shock, Kazam began to shake violently, as if in pain. But there he stayed until slowly, eventually, the letters on the book's cover began to lose their shimmer, then disappeared completely. Whatever the new method was, it had worked.

"*Aha*!" Kazam shouted delightedly, stepping away from *The Tome*. "So all it needed was a sacrifice from me … I should have known … typical Merlin. But I'm almost there."

Marvin's parents were nearly upon him now, wands pointed at the evil wizard's back. Marcus lifted his gaze to where Jack and Pete were trying to free Merlin, so far without luck.

ALAKAZ

Kazam purred gleefully to himself. He began to write his name in the air with his wand, each letter burning in golden sparks before him. Fred watched in awe as the letters then magically started to appear on the binding of *The Tome*.

But before Kazam could finish, Marcus leapt forward, striking the wizard from behind, while Maggie rushed round in front, wand pointing straight at the wizard's chest.

Kazam seemed unbothered by their arrival. "I thought you might appear here eventually," he said. "Did you enjoy the downpour? Quite an enchantment, isn't it?"

"It's over, Kazam," Maggie said. "Tell us how to free Merlin."

A menacing grin spread slowly across Kazam's face.

"Oh, there's no freeing my old friend Merlin. You see we go *way* back – to before the book was even written."

"Strange way to treat a friend, Alan," Marcus said.

Kazam twitched slightly at the use of his first name.

"Well, we're no longer on such *friendly* terms. Not since he betrayed me. Removing my name from the book that *I* helped write here in this very cave, denying my greatness …"

"What is it you *want* exactly?" Maggie said.

"I was hoping you'd ask that," he smirked. "What *do* I want? Revenge, perhaps? Recognition?"

"Recognition? For your terrible crimes? What good's that to you now?"

"Look, maybe I *did* commit some crimes; perhaps they *were* a little terrible. So what? The world needs to know the truth: their *hero*, oh-so-perfect Merlin, is far from it! For too long he's been taking credit for things *we* achieved – *I* achieved! *I'm* the greatest wizard who's ever lived, and should be honoured as such. Not Merlin! Me!"

He paused for a moment before adding, "And I want my favourite teapot back. Merlin borrowed but never returned it. Throw some biscuits in too."

"Well, there's just one problem, *Alan*. Isn't your name just a bit too boring for greatness?" Marcus teased. Fred supposed this was an attempt to buy Jack and Big Pete more time to free Merlin, though it didn't seem very sensible to make Kazam even angrier. "I mean, everyone remembers a name like Merlin. But 'Alan, the greatest wizard who ever lived' doesn't quite have the same ring to it."

Kazam twitched. "Stop it."

"You could always use your middle name?" Marcus continued. "Unless it's something like Colin, of course."

Kazam twitched again.

"Oh dear! It *is* Colin!" Marcus laughed. "*And the award for the greatest wizard ever goes to* Alan Colin Kazam? No, that would never do."

"*IT'S ALAKAZAM, NOT ALAN*!"

The cave suddenly filled with a burst of sparks, but not from Kazam's wand. Fred gasped as he looked towards Jack and Pete only to see they were frozen like Merlin; their spells cast to break the ice had rebounded and encased them instead!

"Oh no!" Cara said, in sudden realization. "It must be Impenetrable Ice! It's incredibly rare and dangerous to conjure, but will rebound any magic used against it."

"There *must* be a spell to break it!" Marvin cried. Fred recognized the desperation in Marvin's voice. He felt it too.

"Only one thing can destroy it: natural magical fire," Cara said. "But that exists only in magical creatures. It can't be conjured by a wand."

"So what do we do?"

"I've got to help your parents. But you stay here, that way if things get worse, you can go and get help!"

As Cara set off towards the action, Marvin's parents, distracted by Jack and Pete's frozen state, failed to protect themselves from Kazam's whooshing wand.

Quick as a flash, his spell hit, and they too were trapped in Impenetrable Ice.

Chapter Eighteen

As fear and anger washed over Marvin's face and panic coursed through his veins, he moved to follow Cara. Fred lunged and grabbed hold of him.

"I've got to stop him, Fred!" Marvin tried to break free. "Let go!"

Fred clung on with all his strength. Despite his own fear, his mind was surprisingly clear. Perhaps Merlin *was* right about worries being useful sometimes. Worrying about what would happen if they made the wrong choice somehow helped Fred to think carefully.

"You can't, Marvin! You're brilliant at magic, but this isn't school – we're not up against teachers or textbooks. Look at what Kazam has done to your parents and the others! That'll be us too if we don't think this through, and we'll be no use to anyone!"

"I can stop him," Marvin mumbled, continuing to wriggle.

"You can't – you heard Cara – not with normal magic! But *we* still might if we work together. We've just got to find a different way. Please, Marv. Trust me!"

Eventually, Marvin stopped resisting.

"What next, then?" he panted.

Fred looked back to the scene in the cave. He couldn't bear the evil satisfaction that beamed from the face of Kazam as he stood over *The Tome.* As Cara tiptoed around, trying to stay out of Kazam's sight until she could strike from behind cover, Fred's eyes were drawn once more to the flickering light dancing across the cave …

"Cara said magical fire exists only in magical creatures …" Fred said, as he traced the fire back to the gargoyles' mouths …

Marvin nodded. "Creatures like dragons, serpents, phoenixes—"

"And lizards!" Fred interrupted, gazing at the stone reptile that sprouted from the wall. "We've got to go back!"

Marvin's expression changed as soon as

'lizards' had left Fred's lips. He knew exactly what Fred meant.

"We'd better be quick!"

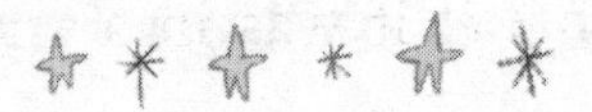

Fred and Marvin sped back down the tunnel. Not knowing exactly which cave they'd sheltered in earlier, they were unable to magic themselves there, but soon they were out in the open, able to retrace their steps. They sprinted along the base of the mountainside.

"Here," Fred said, coming to a halt. He touched the still-hot rock outside the entrance to the cave, scorched by the fire that had earlier missed his bottom by inches.

"Fred, are you sure it won't gobble us up?"

"Yes," Fred replied, trying to convince himself as well as Marvin. He had no idea what the lizard would do, or if it would want to help. What if it was in a terrible mood? And even if it was in a *good* mood, could Fred really win it round again, or *had* it simply been luck the first time round? The only thing Fred knew for certain was that *trying* was their only option. "Come on."

They cautiously tiptoed into the dark cave, a deep, steady rumbling sound echoing around them.

They headed towards the lizard's snores.

The creature was even bigger than Fred remembered. Its enormous middle expanded slowly with each breath and its thick, powerful tail stretched out behind it, twitching as if being used in the lizard's dream.

The first time Fred had met the lizard, it had also been asleep and then he'd done everything he could not to wake it. But now, they needed the creature to wake up, and quickly. So he and Marvin started doing everything they could *to* wake it. Marvin made bursts of water shoot from his wand, fireworks explode, symbols crash and gigantic alarm clocks rattle and ring next to its ears, but nothing stirred the beast.

"Maybe this isn't the time for magic, Marv," Fred said. "Just kick it!"

But after the boys had kicked and poked, thrown rocks from the cave floor with all their might, and even tickled the creature, still the lizard snored on.

Feeling more desperate than ever, Fred suddenly began rifling through his rucksack.

"What are you looking for?" Marvin asked him.

Fred pulled a packet of crisps from his backpack. He looked at the flavour: chicken-and-sweetcorn soup. Not ideal, but worth a try.

"It's not the time for a crisp sandwich, Fred!" Marvin said.

Fred waved the open packet back and forth in front of the lizard's nostrils. "Just watch."

As the smell slowly wafted through the air, the lizard's nostrils began to twitch. Its eyelids started to flutter. Before long the lizard was drooling. Then, with a sudden

CRASH!
BRRINNGG!!!!

jerk of its head, it woke. The boys jumped back.

For a moment, the lizard stared at them, expressionless. Fred worried that at any second the lizard would open its mouth and eat them whole. Then it spoke.

"Oh, it's you! But with … strange ears, and a friend."

After introducing Marvin, Fred formally introduced himself too. He'd forgotten to the first time he and the lizard met. The lizard returned the nicety. Fred hadn't expected it to be called Linda, which didn't seem a very lizard-y name. But then again, what is?

"Well, Fred, I was enjoying that snooze. I don't appreciate being woken up," Linda said. "Especially by people who've disturbed me once already today. I trust it was you in my cave earlier?"

Fred and Marvin gulped.

"It was – we're very sorry about that."

"I should hope so," Linda continued. "It was very rude. I've half a mind to gobble you both up."

The lizard opened her enormous mouth, wide enough to engulf both boys in a gulp …

"No! Honestly! We're *so* sorry," Fred began, thinking how stupid he'd been. "Please …"

"Accept your apology?" The lizard finished her yawn and closed her mouth. "Very well."

And just like that Fred and Marvin were able to breathe again.

"I know you're brave, Fred, but I also know you're not stupid. You must have a good reason to come here. What is it?"

"We need your help." Fred quickly explained all about Kazam, his crimes and the current situation in the cave and how the only way to save the others was using natural magic fire.

"That's why we need your help! We can distract Kazam, while you use your fire to free the others."

"I see," Linda the lizard said, intrigued. "Well, this Alan clearly needs to be stopped. But what's in it for me?"

The boys searched their rucksacks for anything they could offer.

"Er, this pencil?" Marvin said.

"Merlin's polka-dot bloomers?" Fred suggested.

"Some plasters … my wetsuit … this bit of fluff," Marvin continued, pulling out items in a hurry. "Ooh, what about a lifetime pass to the world's greatest theme park, Alton Towers?"

"Or VIP tickets to *Matilda the Musical*?" Fred said.

"This voucher for twenty per cent off all main courses at Pizza Express?" Marvin said hopefully.

"Is it valid on Saturdays?"

Marvin checked. "Only Monday to

Thursday."

"No, then. But I am hungry."

"Well," said Marvin, struck by inspiration, "we can't promise he'll taste nice, but Kazam might be a more interesting meal than you've had for a while."

"Interesting," the lizard said. "I've barely eaten a morsel since Fred's last visit."

"And, for dessert," Fred added, "more crisps than you could wish for."

It worked. Linda licked her lips and smiled.

"Well, in that case, we'd better be off, hadn't we?"

With that, after Fred and Marvin had climbed onto her enormous back, the three of them raced back towards whatever fate awaited them.

Chapter Nineteen

"I'VE NEVER RIDDEN A LIZARD BEFORE!" Marvin screamed, clinging on for dear life as the lizard raced across the craggy landscape. "THIS IS CRAZY!"

"ME NEITHER!" Fred replied. The thrill of the ride was almost helping him forget his fear and he was surprised to be enjoying the moment, especially given the dangerous situation ahead.

The feeling vanished as soon as they arrived back at the tunnel.

"Was it always this small?" Fred said, as the boys jumped off the lizard's back and inspected the opening. "The lizard will never fit through there! What are we going to do?"

"Move aside." Marvin pointed his wand at the tunnel. With a steady hand and unbroken focus, he carefully rotated it. Slowly, miraculously, the opening spiralled and the tunnel enlarged enough to accommodate the lizard's great bulk.

"Not bad, eh?" Marvin smiled.

"Incredible!" Fred said.

"I'm a fast learner," Marvin replied. "Let's go."

They clambered back on to the lizard's back and she ambled down the tunnel. Gradually, faint noises filtered down to them, becoming louder the closer they got to the chamber.

CRACKLE!

POP!

SNAP!

Fred and Marvin climbed off the lizard and peered round into the chamber again. They were amazed – and relieved – to see

Cara wasn't trapped in ice like the others, but instead locked in a spell battle with Kazam. A giant net shot from her wand towards Kazam, who, with a wild flourish of his arm, made it disappear just in time. He fired angry, scarlet jets that transformed mid-air into razor-sharp arrows destined for Cara's head; with a swipe of her left arm she conjured a shield to block them, then threw an upwards spell with a punch of her right. Kazam looked up, horrified, as the stalactites that hung from the cavern ceiling dropped towards him. He dived to avoid their spear-like tips.

As Kazam scrambled for cover behind one of his frozen prisoners, Marvin leaped into the action. He dashed towards the middle of the cave and snatched *The Tome* from its plinth.

"Marvin, be careful!" Cara yelled, obviously shocked to see him out in the open.

That moment of distraction was all it took … Kazam, back on his feet, looked at

Cara with wild fury in his eyes and cast his freezing spell towards her before she had a chance to avoid it. Then Kazam whirled to face Marvin, raising his wand …

"OI!" Fred shouted, "OVER HERE!"

It was enough. Enough to distract Kazam for a split-second, enough to make him hesitate, enough for Marvin to duck for cover from the raging storm of fire that burst from the lizard's mouth, filling the chamber with glorious flames and withering heat.

As quickly as it had encased its victims, the ice disappeared, and Kazam's prisoners were freed from their frozen tombs. Having watched the action unfold they were ready, and pointed their wands at their cowering captor, who'd somehow avoided the worst of

the fire. Merlin was the first to speak.

"Alan, old friend, I underestimated you. I admit it. You won the war, outsmarted and overpowered me. But, thanks to these great friends – and *truly* great wizards, for reasons you'll never understand – it appears you've lost the battle."

"And now it's *really* over," Marvin's mother told Kazam.

This time there was fear in his eyes. Kazam dropped his wand and began walking backwards …

"Alan, you can't escape with magic," Marvin's father told him. "This whole cave has been enchanted."

Still Kazam stumbled backwards.

"There's nowhere to go, Alan," Merlin said.

"*DON'T CALL ME ALAN*!" Kazam cried. Then he turned.

Turned and ran …

… straight into the open mouth of the lizard who was waiting patiently behind him. With a sickening snap of her jaw and a loud gulp, the lizard gobbled up the evil wizard as if he were merely a fly.

"Hmmm," Linda said. "A little bit stale, I'd say. Still, evil wizards often are. Now, Fred, how about some of those crisps?"

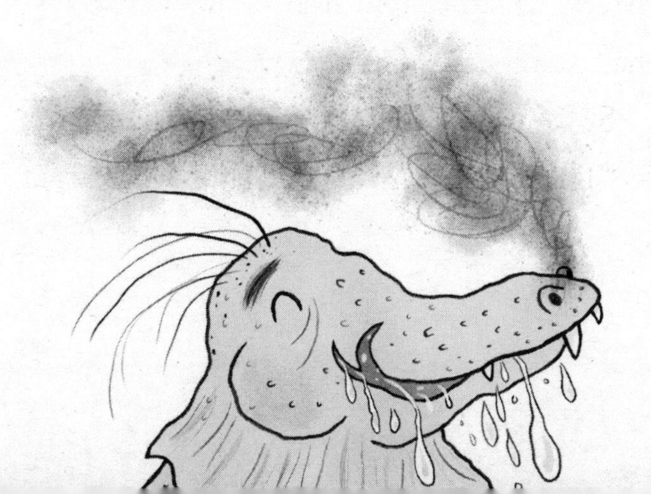

Chapter Twenty

"Merlin, can I ask you a personal question?" Fred said, placing his cup and saucer on the table next to his favourite chair in the great wizard's living room. Despite everything that had happened since their last tea date, they'd managed to stick to their regular schedule. It had taken Merlin a mere flick of his wand to set his house in order again.

Fred found it comforting to see it back to normal, with Merlin – safe and smiling – sitting opposite, but there were unanswered questions that were bothering him.

"Ask away," the old wizard smiled. "Honesty is the least that I owe you."

"What's with all the rubber ducks?"

Merlin chuckled heartily at the unexpected question.

"I suppose I've just always found them most curious. After all, they don't normally do much. I trust you found the ones in my safe?"

Fred nodded.

"Well, when Kazam sent that letter you read, he also gifted me that duck. Being a sentimental old sort, I thought it rather touching. Of course, it turned out to be most sinister. Any fool should have expected that."

"Sinister?"

"He'd enchanted it to transmit my whereabouts, conversations, everything. I'm certain he had an identical rubber duck enabling him to receive such information. Sinister, but brilliant, magic. He knew just how to find me."

"But if he knew where you were all along, why did he wait until now to kidnap you?"

"I think he had been coming up with a plan for some time, but had to wait patiently in hiding until everyone – including those who'd refused to accept it at first – believed he was dead, and he could strike without anyone suspecting. The idea of the exhibit at the museum was what finally pushed him to act. He couldn't bear the thought that I was about to receive such a public honour. Kazam always believed *his* magical accomplishments were better than mine."

"But why kidnap you at all?"

"He needed me to summon *The Tome*. You see, when it was written, we Magicians of Might enchanted it so any of us could summon the book, if needed. But I removed Alan's name long ago, so he found himself unable to summon the book. You saw how desperate he was for recognition, to have his name back on *The Tome* – for which he needed me. At first when he captured me I refused to help him, but then I realized that I could actually use the disappearance of *The Tome* to make sure Kazam was caught."

Fred looked confused. "But how would that help?"

"*The Amazing Ham Maniac.* When I summoned *The Tome*, I replaced it with that book. It was my clue – for you, Fred."

"*You* left it – for *me*?"

"Leaving a more obvious, magical clue would've been dangerous because Kazam would have noticed. But brilliant magical minds often forget the value of the *non*-magical, assuming magic is the answer to everything. I'd hoped U.N.I.C.O.R.N. might see beyond that, to save putting you in danger. Alas, they didn't. But I knew I could count on you."

Fred still didn't quite understand. Merlin smiled his twinkling smile again.

"I imagine you'd hoped our recent get-togethers would involve rather more magical tuition?" he asked. "Sharing some more advanced magic?"

"Only because I need it," Fred explained, not wanting to offend Merlin. He was very fond of their tea dates.

"So, let me ask you: what else have I

taught you?"

Fred thought hard, back to his sessions with Merlin, and finally understood what they'd been about. The magic wasn't important: it was everything else.

"Lots," he said.

"Thank goodness I've not lost my touch!" Merlin joked. "Fred, the reason I left that book is because I knew you'd see it for what it was. I knew you'd think carefully, trust your instincts, be determined in the face of doubt, and *never* give up. None of these qualities require even simple magic, yet I consider them simply magical. You have them all."

Merlin's words filled Fred with pride and, for the first time, he believed them. He'd succeeded *because* of his lack of magic, not in spite of it. This time, there was no reason for him to feel like a fraud for not using magic – that had been the whole point of Merlin's plan! And now he was starting to feel a little bit more heroic too … After all, rescuing a powerful wizard like Merlin was about as *heroic* as things got. To his surprise, he'd actually *enjoyed* the attention of his classmates and teachers at school that day. He and Marvin had spent each lesson enthusiastically answering questions, as everyone was desperate to know every detail after hearing about their adventure on the news. And the banner in the foyer now read, 'WELL DONE, FANTASTIC FRED & MARVELLOUS MARVIN!' which Fred much preferred.

Then Fred remembered something Cara had mentioned; that Merlin had always refused to speak about Kazam and *The Tome*'s chapter on dark magic.

"The chapter on dark magic. Did you—"

Merlin nodded.

"Things aren't always what they seem, Fred. I wrote it – most of it, at least. When we were young, before we knew better, discovering the true scope of magic, good and bad – Kazam became obsessed with power. Dark magic is an intriguing, captivating thing. For a while, I joined my friend on that dangerous path. By the time *The Tome* was written, I'd freed myself from the grip dark magic had on me. I thought I'd freed my friend too. He convinced me to include that chapter to warn of the perils of such magic. Foolishly, I agreed. Of course, he was still under its spell and developed dark magic beyond anything I'd imagined. That was when I removed his name from *The Tome* – something I tried to make impossible to reverse, but which, as you saw, his magic finally overcame – and, hopefully, any link to Kazam and his crimes. I didn't do it to take *personal* credit for *our* successes, but to protect the honour of *The Tome*, the Magicians of Might, and, selfishly, myself. My intentions were good, but yes – I suppose I am guilty of taking credit for achievements that were not *entirely* my own."

Fred let Merlin's revelation sink in. He could see the regret on the old wizard's face.

For the first time in their relationship, he felt like the wise one. Fittingly, an old piece of Merlin's wisdom came to him.

"You're always telling me that a wizard is judged not by the spells in his brain or the power in his wand, but by his choices and courage."

Merlin nodded approvingly.

"And, in the end, you chose the path for good. You've made mistakes, but maybe now you can fix it. Could you erase Kazam's name again, and that chapter from *The Tome*?"

Merlin rose from his chair and walked over to the ancient book. He paused, considering all that resulted from his decision so long ago, before placing his hand on its cover. Fred watched as Kazam's name disappeared and a whole section of the book withered away so it gradually reduced in size.

"That was long overdue," Merlin sighed, removing his hand and turning back to Fred. "I've politely declined the honour the museum wished to give me. Totally unnecessary and unwanted, I assured them. Instead, I suggested they host an event to celebrate what's really important – the return of *The Tome* – and that they honour everyone involved in its rescue. In particular, two brave and remarkable young wizards."

Amazing! Fred thought. He couldn't wait to tell Marvin.

"Now, dear, brilliant friend," Merlin continued, "tell me . . ."

"Yes?"

"Would you like me to fix your ears? I hate to sound unkind, but I much preferred them before."

Fred touched his ears. Among all the drama of the last couple of days, he had forgotten all about Marvin's spell. Everyone at school had clearly been too polite – or uncomfortable – to say anything.

"Yes, please!" he laughed, and with a whoosh of Merlin's wand it was done.

"That's better," he said.

And it was.

Everything was.

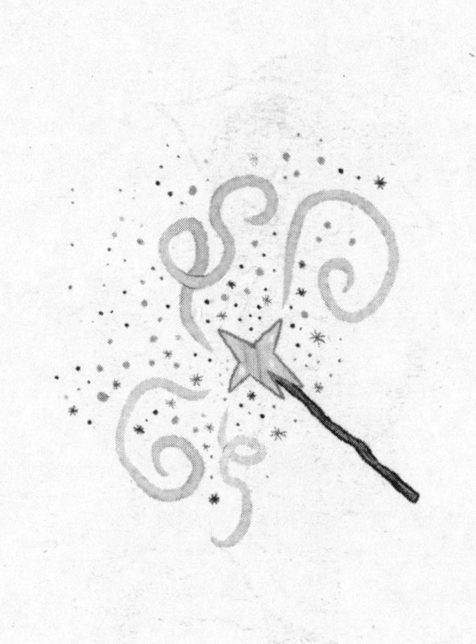

HAVE YOU READ . . .